THIS WALKER BOOK BELONGS TO:

....

....

Anak
50,000
YEARS BEFORE
PRESENT
Maarten
EARLY
1700s
Jalak
MID
1700s
Henry
LATE
1780s
Finola
EARLY
1820s
Bridget
EARLY
1900s
Harry
LATE
1940s
Olga
LATE
1940s

Martha
LATE
1840s
Nianzu
LATE
1850s
Karim
1870s
Marina
EARLY
1950s
Cornelia
1960s
Hau
LATE
1970s
Abdul
2000s

For Simon and Quinn Wentian with love,

and for my family – Rawlins, French,

Tully, Gibbens and Alshammary. DR

For Margaret Georgina Potter.

5 September 1928 – 21 July 2017. HP & MJ

The creators wish to thank

the National Maritime Museum, Sydney, New South Wales;
the Immigration Museum, Melbourne, Victoria;
the State Library of Victoria;
the Lamm Jewish Library of Australia;
the Chinese Museum, Melbourne, Victoria;
and the staff of Bayside libraries, Victoria,
Hawkesbury Central Library, Windsor, New South Wales,
and the Max Webber Library, Blacktown, New South Wales.

First published in 2018
by Walker Books Australia Pty Ltd
Locked Bag 22, Newtown
NSW 2042 Australia
www.walkerbooks.com.au

This edition published in 2021.

EU Authorized Representative: HackettFlynn Ltd, 36 Cloch Choirneal, Balrothery, Co. Dublin, K32 C942, Ireland.
EU@walkerpublishinggroup.com

A catalogue record for this book is available from the National Library of Australia

ISBN: 978 1 760654 45 0

The illustrations for this book were created
with graphite pencil and gouache

Typeset in Goudy Old Style and Pablo
Printed and bound in China

10 9 8 7 6 5 4

DONNA RAWLINS • HEATHER POTTER • MARK JACKSON

waves

FOR THOSE WHO COME ACROSS THE SEA

Anak

WE LEFT WITH OUR COUSINS, aunts and uncles – rafts ahead of us bouncing and tumbling over the waves. And behind us, twenty or thirty at least, following in our wake.

It was not long before we drifted apart. I feared that would happen. And then we were alone.

Our stomachs rumbled with hunger and churned with the waves.

It was no place for Anjing. A dog is not a sailor, but I could never have left her behind. Father said I must cast her off. The dry salty fish we ate made us thirsty, and our water was nearly gone. But mother was on my side, and let me keep her.

We were on the water for days and nights, chasing the gleaming schools of fish into currents we had never sailed.

"The fishing will be good there, Anak," my mother told me.

That is the excuse she gave me for this endless journey.

How can they be so sure there will be land where no one has ever gone? I worried that my father was lost.

He was far too busy with the raft to speak, and I knew he watched the stars all night while we slept.

No human could survive this far away. This will be an empty place with just the three of us until my parents grow old and die and leave me, all alone, at the end of the earth.

My eyes ached from gazing at the horizon – all day, every day. And then, the smoke at the edge of the great wide sea – just a tiny dancing wisp of it rising from a thin green line.

Maarten

ON AND ON WE SAIL, the Captain with his jaw set against the scything wind, the officers with their burden of orders. The sailors, poor and hopeless, like me. The officers' wives coddle their babies, born squawking like gulls and seasick before they reach the breast. We follow the maps to the spices – cloves and pepper and canes of sugar – and the salt of the silvery fish left to age under the sun. We promise to return with ivory.

We have rich cargo and a whole new mint of silver coins to trade. But now, where are we? We sail south, and south, and further south, and south again.

And then – in the horrible biting wind, on the terrifying rocky shore – we crash. There is panic, chaos, shouting, pleading and choking in the briny waves.

Forty. Fifty. I count them, now more – drifting facedown in the roiling foam.

Men. Women. Children half my size. Babies like my little sister. All with their coats and petticoats full of the water that will deliver them to their graves far beneath. They struggle against the grappling undertow.

A little boy, Jacob, flaps his tiny hand and calls to me, "Maarten! Maarten!" but disappears before I can reach him. And then he is gone.

What is this place? Where is the port teeming with traders? I do not belong here. Not in this hot and alien and mapless world.

Jalak

HERE IS MAREGE, our destination, at the end of my first long journey on this lumbering perahu.

The men on the rigging are shouting and excited when they see tamarind trees towering on the horizon. My uncles furl sails and haul ropes and ready the spears and canoes.

At last, here is our prize – the trepang, glistening orange and red in the sands of these shallow, crystal waters.

"Watch, Jalak," my father says. "Lower your spear and strike!" He will teach me to feel for them in the shallows with the soles of my feet, like the island women do. And how to skin and wash them of the bitter taste of coral, and peel the mangrove bark to wrap them in. We will build fires to smoke the slippery creatures, then they will last the long journey home.

Soon my father and uncles will be old, and it will be me, setting sail every year, with the other men. We will load our ships with rice and knives, axes, tobacco, cloth and gin to pay for our catch. And we will return home with our treasure from the distant shore, and be rich and important.

But what if I do not want to risk the deadly sea?

What if I cannot lift my feet out of their pure white sand?

What if I fall in love with the songs I hear there, and the singers who sing them – enchanted like my brother was?

What if, like him, I stay?

LINED UP AT THE LAPPING DOCKS I prayed, for a day, a week, a month, a year of honest work to feed us all. I have all my humble bagging over the one round shoulder. It is freezing, this last morning on land. By miracle I heard the bursar call my name, Henry, and I have secured the promise of a hammock.

There I wrestled for air with four others, but sick I was, all night, in the stomach, and trembling all over. Hot and cold,

with everything departing me at both ends. Pray that this is just a petty fear of the waves. Lord, preserve me from the ague that washes up at our feet in the guts of water rats.

While I sat, waiting for my passage, at the stinking river's edge with my reeling, dizzy head in my hands, I clutched the last tinged-green mother-gift I had to cling to.

"What is that sprig you have there, young lad?" a stranger said.

"Not a sprig – but a promise," say I.

It was just some fragrant leaves, he was right. But it was the last winter green of the last small thing growing near the docks that we grasped, Mother and me.

I had tucked some of the sweet-smelling leaves under my mother's shawl as close as I could to her heart. It was a token of life to promise my safe return.

"You will return to your mother with far more than leaves, young man," the stranger said. "You will grow for her a whole branching tree."

Finola

EVERY TIME I WATCHED THE SHIPS sail past down the stinking river, out into the deep green sea, I wished it was me sailing away. I would go to the continent. I would wear silk against my skin, and not this lousy petticoat. I would eat cake and have cream on my bread.

At least, that is what I planned.

Not this.

All the others are adults, some men, some big lads, but mostly women, damned like me. None of them dare protect me from the seamen ruffians. And they guard their places down below nearest the portholes – shrews, the lot of them. I have been wedged between two stinking fishwives for so many weeks I have lost count.

Why? Because I am stupid, that is why. Stupid Finola Frances O'Dwyer. If I had not given cheek to my mother, if I had not stormed out into the street just as that Kelly girl, Morag, came hurtling towards me, if I had not accidentally tripped her sending her shopping everywhere.

If I had not stopped to help her pick up all those beautiful glass buttons, wondering how in the Holy Mother's name could she afford *those*?

If I was not still holding them, gawping at them, when she disappeared across Liberty Bridge just as the policeman caught up ...

Well, if it was not for all those things, I would not be heaving on this forsaken prison ship sailing to Hell.

But I am.

Martha

MOTHER IS DOWN BELOW. I can hear her from here. Everyone can! Any moment now I will have a little brother or sister – if it lives. Number nine then, number seven still here on Earth. If it is a girl it will be called Mary Ann after this brave ship of our deliverance. If it is a boy, well, I expect Mother will name him after one of the twins, Esau or Jacob, both cherubs now with the Lord. Bless them.

The wind shrieks something fierce. It slaps the sails, and the waves dash over the deck drenching us through. I gather Rebekah, Sarah, Elijah and baby Jeremiah close to me and try to stop their tears. Angel has told them that ships always sink going around The Horn and that we are all doomed to a freezing watery grave. Then she has

flounced off tittering with that girl from the upper deck leaving all the bigger bairns praying and believing her, and wailing, “Sing a hymn, oh please Martha, sing a hymn so God will hear you and save us.”

Whatever were they thinking, giving Angel that name?

Father will meet us at the dock and we will finally see this wild red place he has filled our dreams with, and filled, too, with his precious sheep. We’ll see the gangarus that jump to run, and grunting bears in the trees – if the wind ever settles – if the ship stays afloat – if we ever make landfall – if we live.

Oh damnation. Now I am crying with the babies.

Curse that wicked Angel.

"NIANZU!" ZU FU CALLS ME to the side of the ship. "See there? Do you see, sharp-eyed boy? There is the land we will make our home." I can't see any land. I squint into the distance but all I see is wave after wave and diving white gulls.

Grandfather's trunk is packed with his tools for smoothing and shaping wood into wheels for carts. His wheels are perfect – evenly hewn to glide our cargo of travellers from the dock to the fields where they will rip the earth open for the gold they swear lies beneath. It is nearly one hundred li we must travel, but it will help us pay back the big debt we owe to that greedy agent who gave us passage and the horse.

I will be as old as the ancestors before we get there!

My wheels are no good, not yet. The cart would lurch and hiccup over the rocks. But I will become more skilled at it and when Grandfather is too old, I will take over, and my wife and children will look after him while I work.

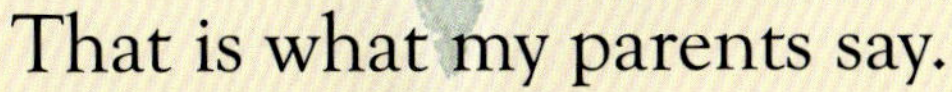

That is what my parents say.

I would rather find rivers of gold and have no wife or children. Then I could be a rich man and sail around the world and back to China in a private cabin with gifts for my parents. I will save Zu Fu's wheel tools in my trunk, though, just to remind me where I have come from, and what might have been.

We'll see.

Karim

"WHEN YOU GO TO THE MARKET, dress in your rough travel clothes. No one will suspect you are carrying so much gold when they see such a scruffy urchin on the road," Uncle's letter said.

His instructions were many. Where to find the camel seller, how to bargain with him, how much to pay him – "not a coin more"– which camels to buy – "Check under the saddles I left with them. I've scratched their names where that rogue won't see and switch them."

I read down Uncle's list and counted them – the last six for the string:

Al Ghab will only need to drink every two days. Take him.

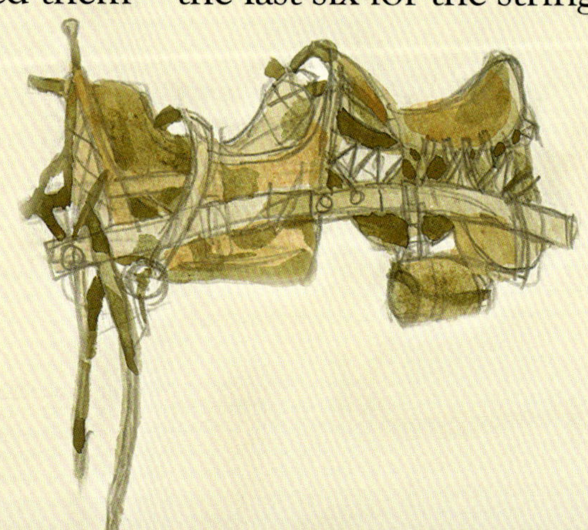

Al Salouf – she will lead the others to water. Take her. Addawser is very big, he will carry good loads. Take him. The list went on. (*"Al Melwah is no good. Don't take him. He can never get enough to drink."*)

At the market one camel wouldn't let me out of her sight. "Al Khlouj, she has lost her baby and cannot be consoled, she pines and will not eat," the seller was honest and told me. "She will die soon."

But when his back was turned she ate hungrily from my hand. He didn't see.

"Take her. For free," he said. "She is no good to me."

Down at the bustling dock I loaded them all onto the ship. I tended them as we sailed from one distant desert to another – across more water than I could have ever believed existed, but all of it made of salt. At least my camels could drink it.

Now I am finally here, Uncle means me to turn around and leave the railway builders' camp and sail straight back to my boring studies, but I have other plans. Now I have my loyal Al Khlouj we can trek wherever we like in this new world far away from all the women at home. Nobody to watch over my shoulder, always treating me like a child. We can be explorers. We will wait until Uncle is asleep, then go.

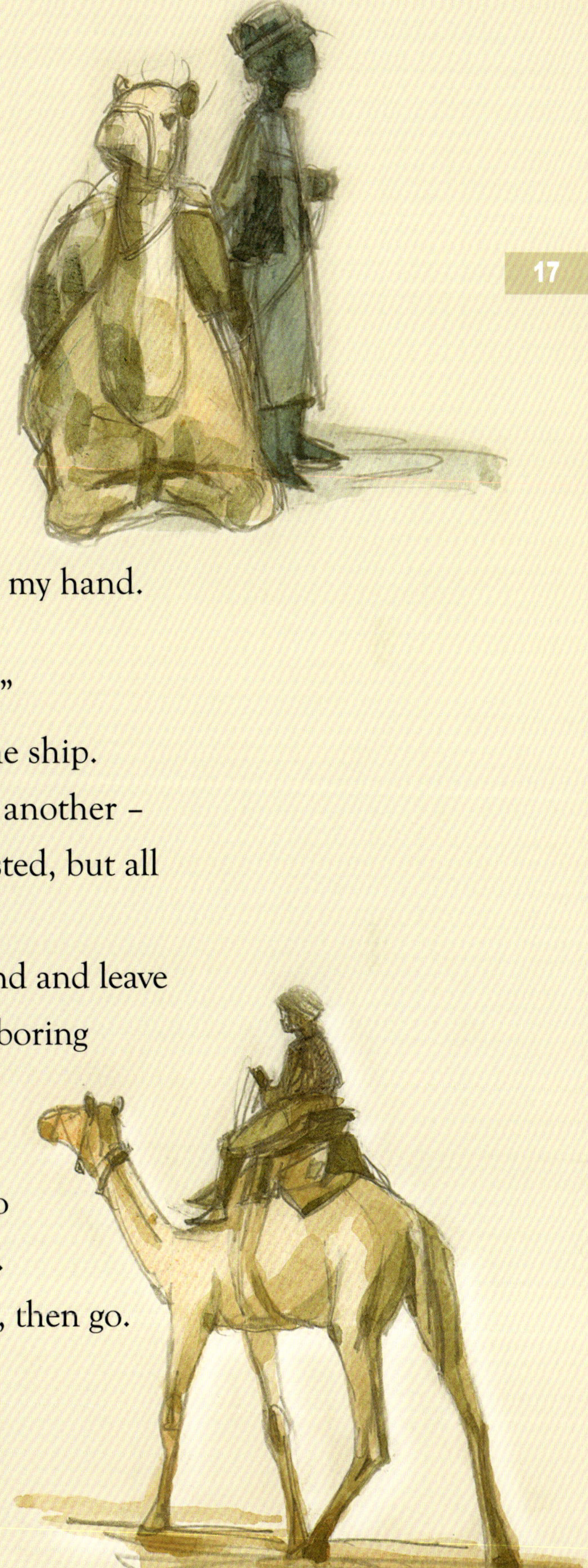

Bridget

ELSIE DIDN'T LOOK RIGHT. She was as white as a petticoat, then red as blood, then like a ghost again. She dragged her little feet up the gangplank when Mama couldn't carry her any more, what with the baby coming so soon.

"Hurry her along now, Bridget Rose," Mama said when Elsie sat down hard on the gangway blocking all of the other passengers. I had to scoop her up and carry her on my back and she was nearly as big as me.

Then, two days later, she was sweating and covered from top to tail with angry red spots. Measles.

At first she held her head and rocked.Then she moaned all night and gabbled nonsense all day. Then, she fell silent. And then she was gone, like she never was – there and then not there.

Mama frets and blames herself through her wailing and fearing for the new baby when it comes. Has she forgotten me?

Another lady is on the captain's deck now with her newborn baby. A boy. And because he has lived, she has named him after the ship and the captain, so his name is Gothic Moorhouse. He doesn't look like a Gothic to me – more a Maxwell, a Cyril or a Roy.

Papa's eyes are red from missing Elsie and he whispers, "How many more days until we reach shore, Biddy?"

"Thirteen," I say, and wince, and cross my fingers behind my back. Five little ones are gone already, and I worry I will be next. I scratch each passing day on the wall next to my bunk and pray. Twelve, eleven, ten ...

Harry

"THIS IS YOUR BIG OPPORTUNITY, Harry," Mr Morrison said at the Chapel gate. "Do this for the Empire, lad. Show them what a man you can be. Make us proud."

All around me on the deck other kids are crying so much they're choking and hiccupping. Some have worked themselves up so much from fear and wailing and reaching out for their mams down on the dock that they've been sick all around our feet and we're only just setting sail!

I don't have a mam any more to see me off and Da hasn't known me since they sent him back from the war. But the boy squashed next to me had to say goodbye to his mammy forever and now he can't speak at all. He's staring straight ahead and his hands make fists by his sides.

The noise is madness – the deafening ship's horn – the seagulls screeching in circles overhead – the little ones pleading for us to turn back ...

This is supposed to be an adventure. That's what they said. We are explorers going to a land of blue skies and wide open spaces. We'll be farmers to make up for all the ones they lost in the war.

We're young men now and there's no need to be mammy's boys any more, they said. This Better Life For All will make us rich. That is why all those weeping mothers on the docks were hurrying their boys up onto the gangplank and into this unknown – For Their Own Good – I suppose.

I put my arm around the shoulders of the boy next to me and read the name on the tag pinned to his coat – Terrance.

He prickles at first, then folds into me like a baby. "Chest out," I say.

Olga

THERE ARE HUNDREDS of families crammed into this rusty hulk. The women and children are separate from the husbands, and other men. All are squashed into dormitories – one bathroom for men and one for women and children, and in the thick sweaty heat below deck, no laundry at all. They mutter to each other about going from one stinking camp to another.

As we sailed, Dr and Mrs Wilk herded all sixty of us orphans together. I cover the twins' ears when Mrs Wilk uses that word. They still don't know.

We are not to speak with any of the other passengers.

Four big girls are in charge of all of the children over twelve.

They whisper-read to the children from the two books we have.

Mrs Wilk picks me. "Olga, you and Gisella keep all of the little ones occupied, the little devils, and for Heaven's sake don't let them up on deck. Keep them quiet!"

I am relieved. I can look after Jacob and Kitty. They haven't spoken since we left. Mr Wilk told us all to keep silent whenever the captain or officers are nearby, unless we can speak French or Italian – anything but Yiddish. We can't.

There are rules about how many of us from the camps can go to this new safe place. Kitty sobs and Jacob whimpers because they think Mama and Papa won't be allowed to come to us when they learn where we are. I want to say they will find us.

Of course! They've waited so long to be back in our parents' arms. I don't want to lie to them, but I'm a coward, so I do.

"They'll find us, bubele. I promise."

SOON WE WILL BE WITH PAPA. Mama fusses more the closer we get. Soon, Marina. Soon!" First she was crying and missing Nonna and Nonno. Now she is so excited I think she'll jump off the deck and swim to Papa as soon as we see land.

He left before us and is working in the cane fields – cutting sugar cane with Mama's big brother, Zio Fortunato. Papa's letters tease Mama. He says Zio's so old now he has a long white beard. I believe Papa. Zio is forty – ancient!

Papa says Zio's name is "Lucky" now. That's an odd name. It doesn't even sound like Fortunato. I hope I won't have to change *my* name.

Zio has forgiven them for putting him in gaol with the other Italians when the war was on. He says war is always unfair, and we must forgive and forget. He has made a home for us there, so far from our village.

"A good home," Zio says.

I have three things with me to keep safe.

One is my last photo of home with my grandparents, aunts, uncles and cousins. I miss them already too, but I miss Papa more. Two is my language. Mama says only some people will know what we mean. I will have to shout loud to make them understand me.

Three is our egg – boiled and dyed red for Easter a long time ago, already kept for ninety-five whole years – way before Mama, and Papa – way even before Nonna and Nonno.

It is handed down.

And then, at last, in five years' time it will be cracked open and the yolk will finally be a precious stone, hard and gold like amber – a stone to polish and wear as a family jewel, generations old.

I must carry this precious egg as though it were made of glass. In it are all our memories.

Cornelia

THE CLOSER WE GET to this new country, the hotter it gets – and it's nearly Christmas! Mama and Papa are really excited; a new country, new home, new friends and a new job for Papa.

Petra was furious. "They didn't ask us about going to the ends of the earth, they just said it. 'We're going and that's that,'" she blubbered. Her face was blotchy and red. And then she saw them – the pictures of the blonde-headed girls draped all over dishy sun-tanned boys. Now she doesn't shut up about those stupid beaches.

For me it is the end of the world. I've left my home and all of my friends. I won't know anyone.

Mama shushes me. She nods towards the thin, silent, motherless kids sailing all alone. "Think yourself lucky, Cornelia. Think yourself lucky."

The film strips they show us on board show deserts, and railway lines disappearing into the dusty middle of nowhere. Kangaroos baking in the dirt, leathery men in battered hats and frumpy women in really old-fashioned clothes whining in a language I'll never be able to understand. I hate it all already.

Now we've crossed the equator and there's no going back. Mama and Papa joined in the party with all the others and threw each other in the pool on the top deck behaving like idiots gallivanting about in grass skirts. Mr Tadixz dressed up as King Neptune with a seaweed beard. What's possessed them all? It was perfectly all right at home. I'm aching for the sound of the foghorns on the cocoa ships leaving the docks. They're the ships I love. Those ships leave, but they always come back.

Always.

Not this one.

THE PIRATES scrambled on deck just after nightfall, shouting and waving knives. I heard them snatch my sister and my mother and wrestle my father over the edge into the sea. He could not swim. I heard my mother and sister screaming and crying as the pirates' boat sped away with them. I hid until there was silence. Hien thought they had taken me too, and cried when he saw me come out from beneath the blankets.

I scream loud into the sky for my mother, my father, my sister.

Hau

Then nothing. I am numb. I cannot sense my heart beating or feel my breath. My head is light. Hien gathers me into his chest.

The sky is as black as the pirates' eyes and as it deepens, billions of stars appear, brighter than I have ever seen. Perhaps, really, I am dead too and I am sailing into Heaven to be with my family.

But then I see first light and I howl at still being alive. There are only seventeen of us left now, adrift.

Unlucky seventeen. The pirates took our fuel. They took our food and most of the fresh water.

The others let me sleep all day. Hien holds me tight as the sun fades again. He promises to be my family now, and tells me a freighter will come soon and rescue us. "Hau," he whispers, "the name your parents gave you means 'full of hope'. You must keep that promise to them."

Just as he says that, I swear, I can just make out the thinnest line of green on the horizon and a spiral of smoke reaching into the sky.

"Đất đai," I say. "Land."

Abdul

MAMA PROMISES we will go to school and be safe to walk on the street there – no bullets. No bombs pounding all night and day.

On the phone Papa says when children cross the road an adult holds a sign and stops all the traffic to let them pass. He says grown-up drivers Actually Stop For Children! Of course, I don't believe him. But it's nice that he is making up funny stories to help me feel better while we wait and wait.

The journey from the terror has been a lifetime. Mama paid a brave farmer to hide us in his truck, under his sacks of dung. Then we stumbled across land for weeks. I saw Mama cry. She left the last of her treasured possessions by the road, too heavy to carry another step.

We pretended through the checkpoint with happy We-are-going-a-long-way-to-a-family-wedding smiles on our faces – hearts thumping, dressed for a party, not for an escape. Then the airport, at last, and flying halfway around the world. Then waiting and waiting in the stinking, teeming camp full of desperate and hollow hearts. Four birthdays already. How many more? Will we finally find our deliverance on this creaking boat paid for with everything we had and my mother's broken heart?

"What if we die? What if we drown in the sea?"

Hussein slaps my leg to make me quiet. "Abdul! We'd have died if we'd stayed," he hisses at me for making it harder for Mama.

She rocks and prays into the west. I know she is ripped in two. I wish she would decide. The soil or the sea. The captain presses her, "Plenty others happy to take your place Mrs."

Papa says all the people from our new country will welcome us and give us new clothes and gifts.

What will he say next? That we are going to Paradise?

Maybe soon we will have our feet on the firm safe soil of our new home, all our troubles over, at last.

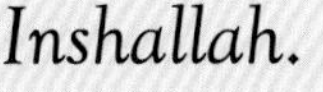

Inshallah.

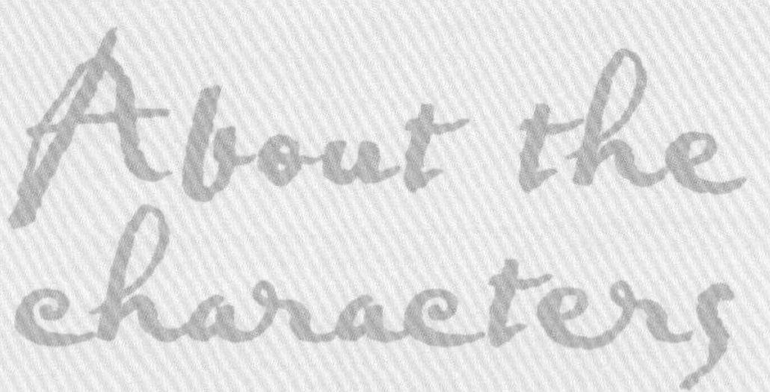

If you are not an Indigenous Australian, your family have, at some stage, come to Australia from across the waves.

The characters in this book are fictitious, but the types of journeys they take in these stories were very real.

Tens of thousands of years ago, **ANAK**'s seafaring ancestors left what we know as Indonesia by raft, settling in New Guinea. Over many generations, his people headed by land bridge and shorter sea trips to coastal northern Australia. Anak, his parents and his dog would have settled in northern Australia, joining those who had already made the trip, over 55,000 years ago.

In 1711, *The Zuytdorp* left The Netherlands, its crew sailing for Indonesia to trade coins for the spices grown there. Presumed wrecked, the ship was lost for many years, until its ruins were discovered over two hundred years later on a remote area of the western Australian coast. Many would have died in the wreck, but there is evidence that others, like **MAARTEN**, went on to live with and marry into indigenous families, becoming among the first Europeans to settle in Australia some seventy years before Captain Cook sailed into Sydney Cove.

JALAK and his people were sailing from Sulawesi, Timor and other nearby islands to trade with the Yolgnu people of "Marege" (northern Australia) for hundreds of years. Some archaeologists say this trade relationship stretches as far back as the 1500s. There is certainly evidence the fishermen who sailed from Makassar in Sulawesi were bringing metal axes and knives, cloth, rice and gin to trade for trepang and pearls in the 1600s, and that the Makassans and the Yolgnu people sometimes married.

In the 18th century, children as young as eight worked in mines and factories, toiling long hours as breadwinners for their families. A boy like **HENRY** might have sailed with the explorer James Cook in the 1770s to send money home and help provide for his family. The youngest cabin boy on *The Endeavour* was eleven years old. That boy, Nick Young, went on to become the servant of the great botanist and natural historian, Joseph Banks. We do not know what happened to him in later life.

Over eighty years, from 1788 to 1868, more than 160,000 people were sent from Britain to Australia as convicts. Many were transported for minor crimes such as theft of food or clothing. On their arrival, most female convicts were sent to work in workhouses or as domestic servants, and single young women were "encouraged" to marry to help populate the newly established British Colony. Some child convicts were orphans, but many, like **FINOLA**, were not, and as they sailed to the other side of the world they said goodbye to their families forever.

In the 1850s manual work was scarce in Britain as a result of mechanisation. Transportation of convicts was winding to a close. Families like **MARTHA**'s were offered land packages and assisted passage as free settlers. Sailing ships took the treacherous "Great Circle" route, sailing far south of the Cape of Good Hope, taking advantage of the wind currents. Encounters with icebergs were common. The voyage took several months – and deaths on board and burials at sea were frequent.

Ancient Chinese records report a map of the entire coastline of Australia dated at 1477, but it wasn't until 1798 that the first Chinese immigrant, Mak Sai Ying, arrived. Then the 1850s gold rush saw large numbers of Chinese immigrants making their way to Australia. **NIANZU** and his paternal grandfather (Zu Fu) might have been some of the first to arrive in the 1850s on the ship called *The Meteor*, or the oddly named ship, *The Land o' Cakes*, berthing in South Australia. Chinese travellers were not permitted to land in Victoria or New South Wales, so travelled by foot 500 kms from Robe in South Australia to Bendigo in Victoria. Of around 40,000 Chinese who came seeking gold, only 4000 stayed permanently.

Australia's enormous deserts daunted European explorers and settlers. Many were defeated in their attempts to traverse, map or farm the continent. In 1860, three Afghan cameleers brought a team of 24 camels to Australia to join the Burke and Wills expedition. Soon after many more cameleers arrived, young men mainly from Afghanistan and what is now Pakistan brought the animals needed to farm the inland and to build telegraph lines and railways. By 1870 around 3000 cameleers, like **KARIM**'s uncle, had arrived with more than 20,000 camels to carry loads such as water, food, wool, furniture and machinery through the vast arid inland.

Like many, **BRIDGET** and her family set sail from the south of England on a journey that would take around six to seven weeks to reach Australia. *The Gothic* left England in December 1912, arriving in Australia in January 1913. Days after departure measles broke out on board, leaving five infants and children dead. Many immigrants had left their homelands for a healthier climate and better work opportunities. Unemployment and poverty had left millions in the United Kingdom and Ireland living in poor housing and unhealthy conditions, so the loss of a child when a family was finally destined to better lives was even more bitterly tragic.

From the late 1800s until the late 1960s, with some short breaks during the two world wars, thousands of children like **HARRY** were removed from orphanages and poor families in the United Kingdom and Malta and brought to Australia under government, religious and private child migration schemes. Authorities in the UK often lied to the children, telling them their parents had died, promising them a better life. In truth, on their arrival, most were used by private and church institutions as slave labour and were often treated with neglect and cruelty. Few of the children, from three year olds up to teenagers, ever saw their families again. The Australian government issued an apology to these forced child migrants in 2009, and the British government followed in 2010.

During the devastating Holocaust in World War II, Jewish people in Europe were persecuted and imprisoned.Six million people were killed in camps such as Bergen-Belsen in Germany and Auschwitz in Poland. Families were split and didn't know who had survived. At the end of the war, surviving Jewish people were resettled worldwide. **OLGA** and her siblings might have sailed on a ship such as *The Derna,* as did a group of 64 children accompanied by two adult chaperones. Australia had set a limit for the number of Jewish refugees it would accept and so some who spoke only Yiddish (the main Jewish language spoken across Europe) remained mute so as not to be found out.

Italy's long history with Australia stretches from early seamen, such as Antonio Pigafetta, sailing with Portuguese explorer Ferdinand Magellan in 1520, who recorded sighting Australia in his ship's log. Another, Antonio Ponto, sailed with Cook on *The Endeavour*. A small number of Italian convicts were brought to Australia, but most Italians were free settlers. Like others, Italians arrived in Victoria seeking gold. More immigrants arrived from Italy throughout the 19th and 20th centuries. Many came from rural villages and were skilled agricultural workers. Men such as **MARINA**'s uncle went north to work in the cane fields, while others grew crops such as grapes further south. During WWII, Italian men were rounded up and imprisoned as "enemy aliens" but were released when the war ended. Many of their families arrived to be united with them, forming a strong and hard-working Australian Italian culture.

Like the Spanish, Portuguese and Italians throughout the 16th and 17th centuries, the Dutch were great explorers, and it is believed that Willem Janszoon was the first European to set foot on Australian land at Cape York on 26 February 1606. There were Dutch among the early convicts and Dutch on the goldfields but after WWII the Netherlands economy was struggling and its government took up the Australian government's offer of assisted passages for thousands of Dutch families like **CORNELIA**'s to come and work in growing post-war infrastructure and industries. Many of the Dutch immigrants were disappointed to find that their circumstances at first were no better, and often worse, than in the Netherlands, but they worked hard to establish themselves and their families in their new country.

In the late 1970s, hundreds of thousands of refugees from the war in Vietnam fled by boat, looking for safe places to live throughout Southeast Asia. Many were tricked into getting on small unseaworthy fishing boats with the promise they would be collected out at sea by larger, safer ships. Hundreds of the boats sunk with the loss of thousands of lives or broke down leaving the people on board stranded with no food or water. People, like those on **HAU**'s boat, fought off attacks by pirates who kidnapped and killed many, stealing their food and possessions. Many of the boats that arrived in countries such as Malaysia and Indonesia were turned back to sea with nowhere to go. Some boats eventually arrived in the Northern Territory and from there the Australian government developed a system to allow the refugees safe airflights to their new homes Australia-wide.

Like so many millions before them, worldwide, **ABDUL**, his brother and mother have been forced to make heartbreaking and dangerous escapes, leaving their homes, their families, their friends and all they know. War, famines and terrorism have left millions homeless and stateless. Those who do manage to reach refugee camps are often left in limbo for years as their refugee status is determined and potential host countries deliberate about who should settle them. Those who risk travelling on boats feel forced into that perilous decision because without necessary travel documents, such as visas, authorities will not allow them to board a plane. Australia is a signatory to the United Nations Refugee Convention. This formal agreement, first drafted in 1951, and signed by 145 countries, sets out to protect refugees and makes clear that asylum seekers must not be returned to danger.

Anak
50,000
YEARS BEFORE
PRESENT
Maarten
EARLY
1700s
Jalak
MID
1700s
Henry
LATE
1780s
Finola
EARLY
1820s
Bridget
EARLY
1900s
Harry
LATE
1940s
Olga
LATE
1940s

Martha
LATE
1840s
Nianzu
LATE
1850s
Karim
1870s
Marina
EARLY
1950s
Cornelia
1960s
Hau
LATE
1970s
Abdul
2000s

FOR THE BEST CHILDREN'S BOOKS, LOOK FOR THE BEAR.

MALLEE SKY
by Jodi Toering
illustrated by Tannya Harricks

An extremely timely and beautiful picture book about the effects of drought and climate change in the Mallee.
The first people of the land call the Mallee "Nowie". It means sunset country. When the sun goes down the red heat of the day bleeds into the sky and sets it on fire. Drought and rain – life under a Mallee sky.

SHORTLISTED, THE CHILDREN'S LITERATURE AWARD, ADELAIDE FESTIVAL AWARDS FOR LITERATURE, 2020
NOTABLE, CHILDREN'S BOOK COUNCIL OF AUSTRALIA BOOK OF THE YEAR AWARD, 2020

"Every brush stroke of this picture book is a masterpiece and every sentence a poetic homage to the sunset country and its strength."
Kids' Book Review

"I was instantly captivated by Tannya Harricks' illustrations in this book . . . blazing sunsets, dreamy starlit night skies, and the dry and dusty earth."
Children's Book Council of Australia: Reading Time

Paperback 978-1-760652-16-6

ONE CARELESS NIGHT
by Christina Booth

Where the mist swallows mountains and winds whisper through ancient trees, a mother and her pup run wild and free. They hunt, but they are also hunted. Carted away. Sold for bounty. And then, one careless night . . .
The last thylacine is gone.

Award-winning picture book creator Christina Booth tells the hauntingly beautiful story of Australia's last thylacine (Tasmanian tiger).

WINNER, PICTURE FICTION CATEGORY, WILDERNESS SOCIETY, 2020
WINNER, CHILDREN'S EDUCATIONAL CATEGORY, WHITLEY AWARD, ROYAL ZOOLOGICAL SOCIETY OF NSW, 2020
SHORTLISTED, PRIME MINISTER'S AWARD FOR CHILDREN'S LITERATURE, 2020
SHORTLISTED, EDUCATIONAL PICTURE OR CHAPTER BOOK, EDUCATIONAL PUBLISHING AWARDS AUSTRALIA, 2020

"I was lucky enough to read this book before its release. I made the mistake, however, of reading it between panels at a writers conference. Halfway through the book, I was sobbing, mascara drizzling down my face – not a great look at a fancy event. But I was still so grateful for the privilege of being exposed to this wonder of a story."
Just Kids Lit

Paperback ISBN: 978-1-921977-00-8

TEN POUND POM
by Carole Wilkinson
illustrated by Liz Anelli

An important slice of Australia's immigration story, detailing the 1960s push for British migrants.

I don't want to go to Australia. I have just started grammar school. My best friend Sally goes there too. But it looks like there could be another war and Dad has convinced Mum to go. Because we're migrants, the voyage is costing Mum and Dad only £10 each.
My brother Brian and I are travelling free.
It's a long way to Australia. What if we never come back to England?

WINNER, PRIMARY, EDUCATIONAL PICTURE OR CHAPTER BOOK, EDUCATIONAL PUBLISHING AWARDS AUSTRALIA, 2018
NOTABLE, CHILDREN'S BOOK COUNCIL OF AUSTRALIA PICTURE BOOK OF THE YEAR AWARD, 2018

"The writing is accessible and compelling; the characters authentic . . . This book highlights a significant chapter in Australia's modern history."
Reading Time

Paperback ISBN 978-1-760653-13-2